an eskimo
birthday

Weekly Reader Children's Book Club presents

an eskimo birthday

Tom D. Robinson

pictures by Glo Coalson

Dodd, Mead & Company

New York

Library of Congress Cataloging in Publication Data

Robinson, Tom D.
    An Eskimo birthday.

    SUMMARY: More than anything else, Eeka wants furs
for her birthday to finish the parka her mother has
made for her.
    [1. Eskimos — Fiction.   2. Birthdays — Fiction]
I. Coalson, Glo, ill.   II. Title.
PZ7.R56764Es   [Fic]   74-23750
ISBN 0-396-07065-5

Weekly Reader Children's Book Club Edition

For the Tikigakmiut: I hope at least
a small payment on a rather large debt.

THE STRONG WIND that had brought the storm shook the windows of the little school with each gust. Often even the lights from the closest houses winked, then disappeared as swirls of snow were thrown against the side of the building.

Eeka kept looking, first at the storm, then at the clock above the blackboard. The hands seemed to be held back by giant weights. Only two-thirty—another whole hour to go! Oh, and it was such a special day! "My birthday," she muttered to herself, as she hit her desk softly with her clenched fist.

Eeka had so hoped everything would go perfectly. It

had been calm when her father had gone out to check his traps early in the morning. Her mother was home cooking a big meal for the party that night, and then there was the beautiful new parka her mother had sewn, complete but for the fur ruff and trimming.

The trapping season had been a poor one, but there was always the chance that this time, especially this time, her father would have luck and find some fox in his traps so the parka could be finished. Now the storm that had completely covered the village with snow took that slim chance away. Eeka sighed and stared out at the darkness caused by the storm and lack of winter sun.

Just then, the door to the classroom opened. The principal came in and whispered something to Eeka's teacher, and when he left, she quietly asked the children to listen.

"Because the storm seems to be getting worse, we're dismissing school early. Many of your parents are out in the hall, waiting to take you home. If your parents are not there, please be careful when you leave. And," she added, "you fifth graders make sure and take home any little ones who live close to you."

Eeka gave a squeal of delight. She threw her books into her desk and went running to the door.

"Eeka! Eeka!" called her teacher. "Slow down before you run over somebody."

Eeka slowed to a quick walk, while one of the other students explained, "It's her birthday and her mother is cooking for her. That's why she's in a hurry."

The teacher was smiling. "Well, happy birthday, Eeka, but save some energy for the walk home! I'd like to see you in one piece for your party."

Out in the corridor, Eeka found her first-grade cousin waiting for her by the coat hooks. Eeka slipped her old parka over her head, pulled the hood up tight around her face, and thrust her hands into the mittens that hung from yarn around her neck.

9

"Come on," she said, taking the little girl roughly by the hand. "Hang on tight, or I'll let the wind blow you away. I'm in a hurry today."

Between the wind and her slippery mukluks, it took all of Eeka's strength to get the school door open. Once outside, the girls were blown sideways several feet by a strong gust before they could regain their balance.

When they were headed in the right direction they both put their heads down and away from the wind that raged against their sides. Eeka looked up only to check that she was going the right way. Each time, the stinging blasts of snow made her forehead ache with cold.

Neither girl spoke. They would have had to shout to have been heard above the wind, and walking up and down the quickly forming drifts didn't leave much breath for talking. Once in a while, Eeka caught the glimmer of a light from one of the houses. Between that and having walked this way hundreds of times before, she was able to keep on a fairly straight line home.

Eeka's cousin lived right next door to her, so, when they got near their houses, Eeka just let go of the little girl's hand and slid down the small drift between the two buildings, stopping with a bump against the storm porch

of her house. Her cousin disappeared inside her door.

Eeka looked for her father's snow machine, but it wasn't there. She stood looking past her house in the direction she knew her father had gone, and wondered how he could ever find his way home in this weather.

Pulling a hand out of one of her mittens, she placed it over her nose to warm it up. With the other hand, she pushed the door open and entered the storm porch.

Inside the long, narrow building, Eeka carefully brushed all the fine snow from her parka and pants. The light from the single, bare bulb on the ceiling made scary shadows out of all her father's hunting gear that hung on the walls. Close by the inside door was a box which housed a female dog curled around her four new puppies. Eeka knelt down and let the mother lick her hand. It was a bad time for the pups to be born, these cold months, but her father wanted to build his team back up. His snow machine was old and a new one just cost too much. Eeka gave each puppy a pat.

Eeka was greeted by the smell of freshly baked pies and cakes as she entered the house, and a loud screech from her little brother. On seeing her, he threw his bottle over the side of the crib and held out his arms to be picked up. Eeka's mother was bustling about the stove. Bending down for a hug, she said, "Happy birthday, little one."

Eeka walked into the only other room of the house, the bedroom she shared with her mother and father. She put her parka on her bed. On her parents' bed lay the new parka her mother had sewn, a beautiful, dark blue velveteen. Eeka had wanted badly to wear it to the Eskimo dance the next night, but the storm had ruined everything. The new snow had probably covered her father's freshly set traps. There was no telling now when the parka would be done, and it seemed enough just to hope her father would make it home all right.

Eeka heard her brother screech again, so she turned with a sigh and went back into the main room to pick him up. Her grandfather was sitting on the edge of his bed in the corner next to the oil stove. He was slowly stripping bits of baleen to use in making the shiny, black baskets he sold at the store. They were small, but they brought a good price when sold at the right time to the right people.

He raised his head and looked at Eeka, his white hair making his wrinkled, brown face seem even darker. Then he looked at the clock, squinting his eyes so that they seemed closed while he read the dial.

"Did they let you out early because it's your birthday?" he asked with a smile. His voice was almost a whisper. "Schools sure have changed."

Eeka laughed as she sat down and began to bounce her brother on her knees. The warmth was beginning to return to her cheeks. "Not because of my birthday, Apah. Because of the storm. A lot of parents were up to get the kids as soon as it got dark." As if to verify her story, the house creaked under a violent blast from the wind.

"I remember coming home from Sunday school once, when I was very little," her grandfather began slowly. He had put his knife down and was looking toward the window. "It was when the Mission was away from town —you know the place—up toward the little lagoon. Anyway, it was stormy like this, and we were trying to follow the row of whale bones back to the village. Somehow we got lost and wandered, it seemed like for hours."

Eeka had heard most of her grandfather's stories, including this one, many times before, but they seemed to get better and better. When other old people came by to visit, they would talk with Grandfather about the way things were in the past. They usually spoke in Eskimo, so Eeka would sit close to her mother who would tell her everything that was being said.

"At first it was fun and then we got scared," Grandfather went on. "We stopped, and some of us started to cry while some of us started to pray. Suddenly, the clouds began to lift toward the south and the wind slowed down. We hadn't noticed the wind when we left the church, or we could have used it as a guide. We were way over on the north beach, almost out on the sea ice. People were looking all over for us. We never knew if it was our praying or our parents' shouting that drove the storm away."

The story made Eeka think of how in the fall, when her family went up to the river to fish, she would miss a couple of weeks of school and join them. Then, after a happy day of fishing and household chores, all would gather around the oil-drum stove in the sod-covered house, and Grandfather would tell the most wonderful stories of all. He would tell of long sled trips and of life when he was a child. He would tell of great feasts, and

of times when there was nothing at all to eat. And he would tell stories so scary that it was almost impossible to go to sleep; about lakes with great fish in them, fish so big they would swallow a man and his kayak whole if he were foolish enough to try and cross them; and of little people who wore nothing but diapers and who would hide behind rocks and cried, just like babies, in the hopes that you would come looking for them so they could kill you! More than once Grandfather had escaped from these "Diaper-People" by the narrowest of margins.

"Well," laughed Eeka's mother, "I'm glad I don't have to worry about Eeka like Grandmother had to worry about you! She would take notice of the wind direction when going out in a storm."

Grandfather chuckled. "I guess children these days are a lot smarter in some things than we were. But," he added, "I'm not sure school gives them all the answers." His eyes were shining.

Eeka wondered if she really had used the wind to guide her, or if she had just known which way to head home from school. There had been buildings on each side of her, and, even if she couldn't see them, she knew they were there and would help her find her way. But to walk home from the little lagoon in weather like this! Impossible!

"It's Eeka's father I'm worried about now," Eeka's mother said softly, as she began to dress the baby. A little frown crossed her face as she spoke. "We'd better hurry, Eeka, if we're going to get those things at the store for tonight. And bring the five-gallon can and the little sled so we can get some stove oil." She slipped the baby up under the back of her parka where he would ride safe and warm.

Eeka put on her parka and went out to tie the can onto the sled. "One nice thing about being a baby," she thought, as her cold fingers tried to knot the rope that held the can on the sled, "is that you get to be packed."

THE WIND WAS at their backs as they walked to the store. Now and then, an extra strong gust would push them ahead, making them run for a few steps until they regained their balance. The light from a snow machine, or the outline of another figure, would appear close by them, then dissolve back into the snow and darkness. It wasn't as cold walking with the wind, but still Eeka and

her mother were happy to see the lights of the new store and the warmth it offered.

Everyone greeted them when they got inside, most people calling out happy birthday to Eeka and kidding her about getting old. Eeka's mother took the baby out from inside her parka. She placed him in the shopping cart, which Eeka began pushing, following her mother up and down the aisles.

The store had been opened only a few weeks, and Eeka was still surprised each time she came in at how much better it was than the old one. Where the old store had been dark and cramped and had only two rows of shelves, this new one was bright and cheerful and looked almost empty, even though it had more things in it. The ceiling was covered with fluorescent lights, and, with the many wide aisles, there was plenty of room for washing machines, racks of clothes, a new snow machine, and freezers full of ice cream and frozen meats.

As they moved down the back row of the store, past the hardware, snow machine parts, and rifles, Eeka and her mother came to the corner where the furs hung. Eeka stared at the five fox skins, all of them small and stained yellow with the oil of the seals the foxes had feasted on. Her mother walked over and looked at each one.

"They're too expensive, Eeka, and not nearly good enough for your parka. There were two others, big and pure white, but they were even more money. Perhaps your father will bring some home from his traps."

"It is probably too stormy for him to find his traps," offered Eeka. "I'll just be glad for him to get home."

They continued on down the remaining aisles. Eeka's

23

mother picked out another cake mix, some tea, and, as a special treat, some frozen fish the store had bought from a village where fish was more plentiful. Eeka knew the guests would like them, and the thought of their delicious taste made her mouth water.

As they walked up to the cash register, Eeka was again teased about its being her "special" day. She blushed and turned away, but she couldn't hide her smile.

The men sitting on kegs and piles of rope near the check-out counter asked Eeka's mother many questions in Eskimo about Eeka's father—when he had left, the direction he had gone, how much gas he had with him, if he had a stove and a tent. Eeka wished at that moment that she'd listened more closely to her grandfather. He had tried to get her to speak Eskimo when she was younger, but she never seemed to have the time. And now, as the men spoke to each other in quiet tones, Eeka understood only that they were discussing a search party.

It seemed impossible to Eeka that in this great, white country one small man, also dressed in white, could be found in such a storm. How she wished he had never gone—and for her!

"Don't worry, little Eeka," her favorite uncle said,

putting his big arm around her shoulders. "If your father's not back soon, we will go out and get him. We won't let him miss your birthday party." He smiled down at her, and Eeka began to feel much better.

It was true, the hunters often knew as much about the movements of one another as of the game they hunted. They knew where Eeka's father had his traps, what trail he would probably take to get back, where he might "hole up" if his machine broke down. They would find him.

THE WALK HOME was horrible! The wind that had pushed them over to the store now blew directly in their faces, some gusts making them stop completely. Both Eeka and her mother put their heads down, not daring to look up. Her mother pulled the sled, heavy with the stove oil and the fish. Eeka carried the rest of the things in a sack clutched tightly to her chest so it wouldn't blow away. Many times they turned their backs to the wind, resting and warming their noses and cheeks with a bare hand.

Whenever they did glance up to get their directions,

the snow flew in their faces and made it almost impossible to see. As Eeka had done when coming home from school, they used drifts, oil drums, dog stakes, and the brief flicker of the light from a house to guide them. Several times they walked around places where they knew dogs were tied, dogs that were now covered with snow and wouldn't appreciate being disturbed.

Finally, when Eeka thought she was as cold as she could get, she saw the familiar shape of her house just ahead. And there, outside the little house, was her father —unloading caribou from his sled. He was home safe! Eeka nearly fell over a drift as she ran ahead to greet him.

Eeka's father had many things to do before he could finally come inside and warm up. First, he carried in a large piece of meat and placed it by the stove to thaw out so it could be used in caribou soup that evening. Then he and Grandfather had to unload the sled and cover the snow machine. Finally, there was the oil to put in the drum alongside the house, and the four older dogs to be fed. Only then was he able to come in and get the hot cup of coffee that would start the wonderful heat flowing back into his body.

All this time, Eeka helped her mother unpack their

groceries, anxiously waiting for a chance to see if her father had trapped a fox. When everything was put away, she crowded near him, but she couldn't bring herself to ask.

Eeka's father spoke to Grandfather, telling him of how he had come across the caribou—three in all—and how the wind had covered up the sound of the machine so that, to the surprise of both the caribou and himself, he had almost run over them. He had grabbed his rifle and quickly shot two of them before they had had time to react. The third had then bolted away into the cover of the storm.

Grandfather slowly unfolded his experience of a similar hunt. As he spoke, Eeka was aware of the twinkle in his eye, the bit of a smile on his face. It seemed it had been while crossing a large bay farther south. It was very foggy and he and his hunting companion had stopped to rest their dogs. Suddenly, very close by, they heard the sound of many caribou slowly making their way across the ice. Every once in a while, one would appear out of the fog, much like a ghost, and within easy range of their rifles. The fog seemed to deaden all senses, and, without a wind to carry the scent of the hunters to the rest of the band, the caribou never panicked. It wasn't until the two men had shot eight of them, all the while sitting calmly on their sleds, that the rest of the herd took notice that something wasn't right and ran off.

"All my traps were covered by the snow, Eeka." her father said. "There was a bit of fur in one trap where a fox had been, but I think a wolverine beat me to him. Maybe he thinks he's found somebody who will feed him and return to the trap. The next thing he'll know, he will be a pair of new mittens for you, as punishment for having taken your fox." Eeka tried to smile, but it was hard not to look disappointed.

EEKA," called her mother, "come and feed your brother. There is much to do before the party and it is almost time for people to come." Eeka was glad to be busy rather than have time to think about something that couldn't be helped. In fact, she was so busy that she was surprised when the door opened and the first of the guests walked in.

By the time all the people had arrived, the last cake had been iced and the caribou soup was done. Eeka and her mother laid a cloth out on the floor and put the food and dishes on it. People could help themselves, and eat either sitting on the floor or on one of the benches at the table.

Eeka and her friends took their plates into the bed-room, away from the adult talk about hunting, prices at the store, the bad trapping season, and happenings in other villages.

The girls laughed and joked a lot while they ate. They talked of clothes they wanted to order and things that had happened at school. They made plans to rush through their chores after school the next day so they would have time to meet at the Coffee Shop before the Eskimo dance,

to listen to records and watch the men play pool. And constantly they were up, chasing boys and younger children out of the room. It was only when Eeka looked over at the unfinished parka on the bed that she thought of the one flaw in this best of birthdays.

When her mother called her to come open her presents, the girls began teasing about what they had brought. Eeka didn't like the idea of standing up in front of all the other people, but she was anxious to see what she had gotten. So, she pushed and shoved with the rest of the girls as they rushed, laughing, into the other room.

Most of the people had brought bowls and sacks to take home the left-over food, and so it was a simple matter to stack the dirty dishes next to the counter where they would be washed, fold the cloth up, and put the presents down in the middle of the room.

Everyone had brought something, either an envelope with a card and money in it, or a present wrapped in a paper sack with a birthday message written across the outside. Eeka's mother insisted that she read every one before she opened it. Some were serious and some, like the message from her uncle, made people laugh until tears ran down their faces.

There were more things than Eeka had ever hoped to get—clothes from the store, a game, a deck of playing cards, a scarf knit by an aunt, a beautiful pair of caribou mukluks from her grandmother, and almost ten dollars from the envelopes.

Eeka was gladly just about to give up her place as the center of attention, when one of the women walked out of the bedroom and held the new parka up to Eeka.

"Here," she said, "put it on so everyone can see the fine present your mother has made for you."

Eeka stared at the parka. Without a ruff or trim it looked anything but nice. It was so lifeless! "Why?" thought Eeka. "Everything was going so well. I hate that ugly thing! I hate it!" But she blindly shoved her hands into the sleeves and stood there, head down, while everyone commented on what a fine parka it was.

Suddenly, she could stand it no longer. Eeka turned to rush from the room, to take the parka off and hide the tears she knew would come if she had to hear another word.

She almost knocked her grandfather down as she spun around. He had left his place on the bed and had silently made his way to her side. He was holding a sack in his hand, which he gave to Eeka.

"Here," he said quietly. "They aren't very good, but it was all the store would give me for one of my little baskets."

All was silent as Eeka opened the sack and looked inside. Slowly, unable to believe her eyes, she pulled out two of the most beautiful white fox skins she had ever seen. They must have been the ones her mother had spoken of at the store!

Immediately, everyone began talking about what fine skins they were—surely the best taken that year! They were passed from hand to hand, so much so that Eeka feared all the fur would be rubbed off. The women discussed how best to cut them to get the most trim and biggest ruff, while the men talked about their whiteness and who had trapped them.

Grandfather sat on the edge of his bed, holding a cup of tea and looking at the floor. The only sign that he heard the remarks about the skins was his smile—a smile that showed how proud he was.

And after being asked time and time again to tell how he had gotten the skins into the house without Eeka knowing, he related the story, quietly in Eskimo. He told how he had gone to the store the day before the

37

party and how he had carefully hidden the lovely, full furs under his bed so no one would learn of his secret.

The rest of the evening was a blur to Eeka. She remembered holding the fox skins and rubbing the soft fur against her cheek.

On her way to bed, she stopped by where Grandfather lay. He seemed to be asleep, but Eeka knelt down beside him and whispered, "Thank you, Apah. Thank you very much." The old man put out a hand and touched Eeka gently on her head. He was smiling, his eyes closed, when she left him.

The last sound she heard, before drifting off to sleep, was her mother humming an old, old song as she swiftly cut up the skins and sewed them onto the new parka.

AUTHOR'S NOTE

This story takes place in Point Hope, a village of approximately 360 people on the northwest coast of Alaska. The characters, like the story itself, are fictional, though some of the stories Grandfather tells are true stories told to me by people in Point Hope.

Point Hope is a village of electric lights, a telephone on which you can call any place in the world, a big new store, snow machines, and mail service (by plane) up to five times a week — weather permitting!

But it is also a village of dog teams and seal hunting, polar bears, a Christmas feast that lasts a week and includes some dances older than the oldest man — older than the oldest man's father — and spring whale hunting when the men go out in skin-covered boats to catch bowhead whales up to fifty feet in length for their meat and oil.

Point Hope is both the old and the new — young and growing, ancient and solid. There are some old people who speak very little English and who wear tennis shoes, and young people who speak very little Eskimo and wear caribou mukluks.

It is, perhaps, the best of both worlds.